SURFERS

Operation Terror

Margaret Mahy

Illustrated by
Ron Tiner

PUFFIN BOOKS

PUFFIN BOOKS

Published by the Penguin Group
Penguin Books Ltd, 27 Wrights Lane, London W8 5TZ, England
Penguin Books USA Inc., 375 Hudson Street, New York, New York 10014, USA
Penguin Books Australia Ltd, Ringwood, Victoria, Australia
Penguin Books Canada Ltd, 10 Alcorn Avenue, Toronto, Ontario, Canada M4V 3B2
Penguin Books (NZ) Ltd, 182–190 Wairau Road, Auckland 10, New Zealand

Penguin Books Ltd, Registered Offices: Harmondsworth, Middlesex, England

First published 1997
6

The moral right of the author and illustrator has been asserted

A Vanessa Hamilton Book

Filmset in Bembo

Made and printed in England by Clays Ltd, St Ives plc

British Library Cataloguing in Publication Data
A CIP catalogue record for this book is available from the British Library

ISBN 0-140-38774-9

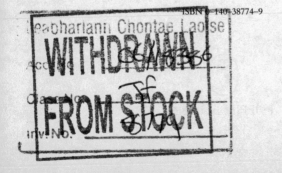

Contents

Chapter One
The Car

"LOOK!" SAID HARLEY.

"What?" said David.

"There!" said Harley.

They had come to a standstill under a street light between the smudgy brick walls and broken windows of Forbes

Street. An upstairs window suddenly shone out like a jagged star of dirty gold, and, looking up at the stab of light, David saw the bricks below it were striped with graffiti. *Where's Quinta?* someone was asking over and over again. The senseless question staggered from wall to wall in black sprawling letters.

It was because of Harley they were picking their way through such a dangerous part of town.

"It'll be an adventure," Harley had said. "Forbes Street's supposed to be really wild. Some people say it's haunted. Glue-sniffers are scared to go there. Even the *police* are afraid."

But Forbes Street was not wild . . . merely poor and dirty. People were what made a city dangerous, and Forbes Street was deserted. Yet there must have been someone around somewhere because Harley, standing under a street light, was staring at a car . . . an ordinary, battered, smeary, blue car.

"Maybe it belongs to a drug dealer," David suggested in a sarcastic voice.

"No! Look! *Really* look!" hissed Harley impatiently. "He's left the keys in it."

Sure enough, there, dangling from the instrument panel, was a round silver ball on a silver chain. It seemed to wink at David.

"Hey?" said Harley. It was just one word, but he was asking David a big question. "What about it?" he was saying.

Over the last six months, ever since his mother, the school music teacher, had run away with a jazz guitarist, Harley had become more and more determined to live dangerously. The trouble was that he wanted David to live dangerously with him.

"Forget it!" said David, staring at the swinging silver ball. *Wink! Wink! Wink!*

"Why not?" Harley persisted. "Whoever owns this car is so stupid, he *deserves* to lose it. It would be *good* for him; he'd take more care of it in the future."

"Forget it!" David said again. "Anyway, who'd drive?"

"Oh, *you* wouldn't have to," cried Harley scornfully. "I'd drive. I'll bet I could drive this thing and the crate it came in."

"Yeah, but any cop who sees us will know we're only kids," said David, immediately irritated with himself for sounding so cautious – so *dull*. He didn't

4

dare say that he wanted to go straight home — that his mother would already be worrying. Harley, his hair sticking up like the crest of an excited cockatoo, was daring — free.

"My uncle showed me how to drive," said Harley. "He said I could drive better than most of the jokers he knows."

"You could be the best driver in the world," said David, "but some cop would still stop us. You're only thirteen and you look about eleven. It's something to do with the way your ears stick out and your hair sticks up."

"Oh yeah, yeah, yeah!" mumbled Harley, trying to flatten his hair. He hated being reminded that he was small. "If we're cruising along, not breaking any rules, no cop'll even look sideways at us."

And he grabbed the handle of the door on the driver's side.

The door opened so obediently that it actually frightened David. Things just weren't as easy as that in real life . . . or they shouldn't have been.

"See?" Harley muttered, sliding into the driver's seat.

David could not resist. So what if they did get into the car for a minute or two? They could always get out again.

"Wow!" said Harley, squinting at the shelf below the instrument panel. "Not just tapes. CDs! Great!"

Then he put his hand on the key. The silver ball on the end of the chain swung slightly, seeming to glance from one boy to the other.

"It's *watching* us!" exclaimed David.

"Come on, Harl! Let's split, or we'll be in big trouble."

"You've got to get home to Mummy, do you?" said Harley contemptuously. "Is it getting too late for you? Or maybe you're scared of *ghosts*?" He was always accusing David of being frightened of ghosts.

Then Harley twisted the key. The car started up, running so smoothly that David had to listen hard to be sure it really was going.

Harley released the handbrake. The car slid forward. David sat back and said nothing. Harley changed gear. They were really moving now, gliding faster and faster between dingy brick walls.

The words *Quinta! Come home!*, sprayed on the bricks in luminous green paint, flashed past. But David barely noticed them. He and Harley had stolen a car. From here on in, they were men on the run.

Chapter Two
"Dilly, dilly, come and be killed"

"Let's have some music!" cried Harley, gripping the steering wheel tightly.

David squinted at the panel in front of him. One of the buttons said CD, and he pressed it.

"You've got to shove a CD *in* first!"

Harley cried, but music was already pouring out from every direction. Some rock band was really letting go – guitars, amplifiers, keyboards, drums . . .

"Cool!" yelled Harley, as David strained to make out the words. Partly because he already knew them, he managed to make them out.

"*Dilly, dilly, dilly, dilly, come and be killed,*
For you must be stuffed, and my customers
    be filled."

David's finger shot out to hit the stop button.

"What did you do that for?" asked Harley crossly.

"Didn't you hear what they were singing?" David asked.

"Nah!" said Harley. "Good beat, though. Put it on again."

As the music played they had been sliding slowly and smoothly through decaying streets. Now, they were out on a well-maintained one-way system . . . familiar territory.

"Don't speed, or they'll pick us up," David said.

"I'm not speeding!" exclaimed Harley impatiently, but somehow he sounded a little less sure of himself than he had only a moment earlier. He looked small in the driver's seat . . . as if he could barely see over the steering wheel. "What was so mind-blowing about the words, anyhow?"

"It was about death," David said.

"Is that all?" Harley said. "Anyone would think you were scared of death. Or, maybe, believed in ghosts."

His left hand shot out to jab the CD button.

"Let's have that music again."

Music filled the car once more, but this time the voices were the pure sound of some wonderful choir. Yet the words of the song were the same — or almost the same.

"Dilly, dilly, dilly, dilly, come and be killed,

For you must be un*stuffed, and my customers filled."*

"Great counter-tenor!" Harley said in a suddenly gentle, appreciative voice. And then, in more normal tones, "Freaky words!"

"Too freaky," said David. "And they've changed one of them. Stop the car. I want *out*."

Harley made the noise of a chicken clucking.

"OK! So I'm chicken!" said David. "Just stop."

He heard Harley's feet move confidently. There was a pause, followed by anxious shuffling.

"What's wrong?" David asked sharply.

"Nothing," Harley replied, his voice sounding high and tight. "No worries! Just that . . . well . . . since you're such a mate of mine, I'll run you home."

"First turn left," said David.

But Harley drove straight past the first left-hand turn, and then the second.

"What's wrong?" David cried.

"Nothing," Harley replied again, but his lips were curled back from his teeth in a terrible wince of fear.

Ahead of them, traffic lights turned red. Harley neither stopped nor slowed down.

13

They sped through against the red, and a car, shooting towards them from the right, gave such a blast on its horn that David's head rang with the sound.

"You're mad," he yelled at Harley. "Stop! Stop, now!"

Harley stared at him, panting a little.

"Watch the road! Watch the road!" screamed David.

"I don't have to," Harley said in a strangled voice. Slumping back in his seat, he took his foot off the accelerator and held his hands away from the wheel. The soft hum of the car's motor did not decrease. It did not lose speed. If anything, the car seemed to move faster than before.

"It's driving itself," Harley said.

Chapter Three
Willesden Forest

DIRECTLY AHEAD OF them, a glowing ribbon cut through the night on the edge of the city. The motorway! The car seemed to surge forward as if it were eager to show them what it really *could* do on an open road. It selected the inner lane, and then accelerated. The hum of its engine deepened into a whispering roar that seemed to carry its own echoes.

"Man!" shrieked Harley. "What sort of car *is* this?"

"I *told* you to leave it alone," David shrieked back.

"You got *into* it, though, didn't you?" Harley sounded as if he might weep. "It's *taking* us somewhere," he wailed. "Where?"

"I reckon it's some . . . some police thing," David said. He knew he was inventing. "A trap of some kind!"

He stopped and stared wildly at the motorway flickering past them. They were being carried *out* of the city. Strange and bleak under its great night lights, the motorway was unrolling into the country. In artificial light, the trees planted beside it looked artificial too, like alien structures put there to fool gullible travellers. The car sped on.

"Willesden Forest," David read on a great sign that now came rushing towards them. "Turn-off two hundred metres."

"Willesden Forest?" yelled Harley. "That's just *trees*, isn't it?"

"It's a government forest," David said, trying desperately to work out what was happening. "They started doing a programme on genetically-altered trees . . . special quick-growing ones." He remembered something. "It's run by the forestry department – well, it *used* to be the forestry department. But the government partly privatized it, and some scientific company is running it for them . . . some big international group . . ."

"I don't care who runs it," Harley yelled. "I just want to go home. I'll be good for the rest of my life."

As he said this, they swung off the motorway on to a long, straight road, sealed and fenced on both sides. Black hills pushed up towards the sky, blotting out the starlight. Willesden Forest loomed over them. Somehow, it felt as ancient as the forest in a fairy tale even though the trees had been planted less than twenty-five years ago. David feared it was about to fall forward to bury them for ever.

Chapter Four

The Experimental Station

WILLESDEN FOREST BEGAN with row after row of pines lined up like ballet dancers. Each tree had its lower branches trimmed away so that it stood poised on one grey leg, green arms upraised, and a stiff green skirt fanning out around it like a ballerina's

19

tutu. Some of the blocks were signposted: EXPERIMENTAL BLOCK A 46.

"I feel sick," moaned Harley.

David felt sorry for him, knowing as he did that Harley's toughness was faked. Deep down, the world frightened him and he had to overact to make himself believe he wasn't scared. And then David thought how completely terrified he was himself. But that was different. He was used to being alarmed by life, and everyone knew it. That was why Harley frequently accused him of believing in ghosts.

On and on and on! The car sped down a straight road that must have been at least three miles long. Then another line of hills rose up before them and one hill thrust out a great black elbow, nudging a crooked curve into the road.

They took the next bend at such speed that the whole forest seemed to tilt around them. Then they swept up and over a rise, only to find themselves looking down on a glowing village . . . long, low buildings and streets as straight as if they had been ruled, with one building rising above the rest like a cylinder of silver. This whole built-up area was contained by tall fences of wire mesh and steel pipes, and the road directly ahead of them was blocked by huge gates.

WILLESDEN EXPERIMENTAL STATION said a notice on the gates. David felt for a second or two that *he* was standing still while the words rushed at him out of an invisible screen.

"We're going to crash," screamed Harley, hurling himself sideways and clasping his arms over his head.

But the gates — like the gates in a fairy tale — swept open, and the car shot into the complex beyond without the slightest lessening of speed. It turned left, then right, passing blank windows and doors that looked as if they were sealed in some complicated electronic way.

"It's going to be all right," David said to Harley. "The car's programmed to come back home to the people who . . . who invented it. I mean, we'll probably get into trouble, but nothing worse than that. Nothing . . ." And here he stopped. Just for a second or two back there he had believed he was going to die.

The car slowed a little. It turned to the right. Directly in front of them was yet another steel fence, a compound contained within the main compound, and behind this second, smaller fence rose the huge, silver-white cylinder of a building they had seen earlier, looking like a blunt spaceship, pinned to darkness by narrow beams of light.

Something moved. The gate to the silver-white cylindrical building was guarded. A man had suddenly appeared and was watching them as the car rolled towards him.

David felt huge relief at seeing another human being in this zone of machines and geometric buildings. It was worth the prospect of an official telling-off and an angry phone call to his parents – worth it to be back in the safe world where someone else knew best.

The guard must have pressed a button or pulled a lever, for the gate opened. As the car slid slowly past him, David saw, briefly, a cheerful moon of a face beaming in at them. The car rolled on by. A door in the building directly ahead of them was already swinging upwards, and then, as the car slid into a slot of darkness, swung down again, closing tightly. The car sighed, inching forward, then came at last to a standstill.

Chapter Five
The Girl

IMMEDIATELY, LIGHTS CAME on. They were in a square white box, so neat and pure it seemed hard to realize it might be a mere garage of any kind. The sound of music came faintly from somewhere, but to David's great relief there were no voices.

Then, as David stared, parallel black cracks appeared in the white wall directly in front of them and not one but two doors opened. The two black spaces in the white wall seemed to issue opposing orders. "Go through *me*!" each door seemed to be commanding.

As Harley opened the driver's door, music came roaring in to engulf them.

"I'm not getting out!" said David.

Harley immediately shut himself in again, and the music out.

"Oh, come on!" he begged. "What are you scared of? Ghosts?"

"Electronic ghosts," David muttered. "Suppose we hit some security system that *vaporizes* us."

"You said they do *forestry* research here," said Harley uneasily. "That's *trees*,

26

right? They won't be worrying about *tree* security . . . For all we know, they'll just tell us off, and then drive us back on to the motorway and turn us loose. I'll bet that's what they do."

David was amazed at Harley's optimism.

"You're just unreal," he said wearily. "I mean, think of this car. It's not just an average old taxi, is it? It's weird. The whole place is weird. Let's . . . let's just . . . just make a *plan*."

They both flopped back in their seats, studying the black doorways in front of them. Then, as they stared blankly ahead, someone appeared in the left-hand doorway.

At one moment it was empty. At the next, someone was *there*, looking back at them.

They could see her in perfect detail – a girl of perhaps sixteen or seventeen, a little hunched, hugging a disintegrating leather jacket that came almost to her knees. Her hair, dyed bright red, was cropped close to her skull. Big, dark glasses with metal rims hid most of her face, but she wore three rings in her right ear and one in her left nostril. She was certainly not the kind of person you would expect to find in a forestry research establishment.

The boys stared at her, and she stared back at them. Then she must have stepped back as quickly as she had stepped forward. David had no impression of her turning and walking back into the darkness beyond the door, but somehow she just wasn't there any more.

"Hey!" said Harley. "Some chick!"

David could tell that the sight of this girl had somehow lifted his spirits a little, and that he was trying to play it cool again.

"OK!" said David, giving in. "Let's face the music."

"What music?" asked Harley. "The Mozart?"

"Oh, ha ha!" said David. "There's bound to be some music, isn't there? I mean, we did sort of *steal* this car."

"It stole us," cried Harley, sounding almost pious. "And anyhow, anyone who leaves a car with the keys in it is *asking* to get it lifted."

Harley's words bothered David. It was true. The car had seemed to be almost begging to be stolen.

And then someone tapped on the car window.

Chapter Six
Winnie Finney

HARLEY LET OUT a small shrill cry that reminded David of a cheap alarm clock. David didn't blame him for shrieking. He would have shrieked himself if his throat had not been totally paralysed by terror. The knocking was about seven centimetres away from his ear. Turning, he looked into the beaming moon-face of the guard who had waved them through the gate. He must have come through some unseen door, and now he was peering in at them, still smiling.

Scrambling out of the car, David on one side, Harley on the other, they crouched, ready for anything, even attack. The man, though, looked entirely friendly. The air around them still rang with piped music, but it seemed quieter than it had been when Harley first opened the car door. Half listening, David realized it was classical music.

"Great run!" the man said, patting the car affectionately. "Nice to meet you at last, though I feel I know you already. I've been monitoring your approach. My

31

name's Finney – Winston Finney. Winnie Finney, they call me. So how did you enjoy your million-dollar ride?"

"Amazing," said David. At least he tried to say it. He felt his lips moving but no sound came from between them.

"Wicked!" croaked Harley, valiantly trying to be cool.

"I, personally, took it through its imprinting run," said Winnie Finney fondly. He patted the car's battered flank. "And I tuned and set up the guiding beacons. Well, though we call them beacons they're so small no one knows they're there. Not to mention the latest Japanese technology in the distance sensors, *and* in those bumpers. Touch-sensitive, even at speed! But I mustn't blind you with science. Let's concentrate on getting you two hooligans sorted out. This way!"

David and Harley grinned rather foolishly at each other as they followed him through the right-hand door. Their reception wasn't nearly as bad as they had imagined it might be.

Entering a lift, Winnie Finney pressed a button. David craned to watch, determined to be sure just which floor they were being taken to. But these buttons had no numbers, and it was impossible to tell how fast or how far they were going. All he could be sure of was that they were going down.

"Long way?" he asked, hoping to find out just how far they were actually going.

"Oh, yes," said Winnie Finney. "There's much, much more to us than meets the eye, you know."

The lift stopped and the door slid sideways. A white corridor curved away to either side.

"I'm afraid you won't be able to go home quite immediately," Winnie Finney said apologetically. "But never mind! I'll take you to a place where you can have a cup of coffee and put your feet up."

"Will I be able to ring my mother?" asked David. The thought of coffee had reminded him of his mother. She would be waiting up for him, drinking coffee, and trying not to worry, but growing more and more unhappy with every passing moment.

Though Winnie Finney patted his shoulder, and spoke in a comfortable voice, he did not actually answer David's question.

"Only the most important people ever get down to this level," he said. "You're being treated like celebrities."

He pushed his hand into his pocket and pulled out something that looked to David like a gun. However, there was no bang when Winnie Finney pressed the trigger, merely the sound of a lock unlocking. A door swung open.

"Quickly!" said Winnie Finney, and he pushed Harley and David ahead of him. His long arms were held out to either side in case either of them should decide to break away and run for it.

"Sorry to hurry you, but an alarm goes off if that particular door doesn't close within the minute," Winnie Finney told them. "Security!" he added, as if that explained everything.

They passed along a narrow, bright passage and came out into a second corridor painted in pale blue and curving rather more tightly than the one they had just left.

Half a dozen people were moving rapidly towards them from the right, led by a man and a woman both wearing pale-blue overalls and jackets. Behind this pair walked three rather elegantly dressed people. One of them was propelling an electric wheelchair in which sat a bony old man wearing what looked to David like a kind of oxygen mask.

It was an unexpected sight, even in this place. Winnie Finney seemed surprised by it too. He exclaimed to himself, then flung out an arm.

"Stand back! Let these people pass," he said softly, but sharply.

"We'll make everything as comfortable for you as we possibly can, Mr Yee," the woman in blue overalls was saying as they advanced. One of the three people answered in a language David did not understand. He seemed to be translating the woman's words aloud, perhaps to the man in the wheelchair. None of them glanced at Winnie Finney and the boys as they swept past.

"We specialize", said Winnie Finney, once this group had retreated around the curve of the corridor, "in developing . . . oh . . . aids of various kinds for people who have suffered accidents . . . who can't get around as easily as you or I do. Now, then! This way. You both look rather disreputable, but never mind. You'll have a chance to tidy yourselves before you meet Doctor Fabrice."

"Doctor who?" asked Harley.

"Oh, no! Not Doctor Who," said Winnie Finney, beaming as if Harley had made a good joke on purpose. "Fabrice! A very talented man. Highly thought of in intellectual circles."

"Really, we just want to go home," said David as politely as he could. "And I want to ring my mother." But Winnie Finney was pointing his door-opener at a door which obediently swung open. Skipping to one side, he gestured them in.

"If you just wait here," he said, "I'll have someone with you in two shakes of a lamb's tail. You'll probably have to take a few tests and fill out some forms. Security!"

"*We* aren't security risks," said Harley quickly.

"Ah, but you aren't particularly reliable, are you?" said Winnie Finney. "You can't be, or you wouldn't be here in the first place."

"We're sorry," said David. "It was a big mistake. Can't we just–"

"The difficulty about a place like this is that we have to be so very security conscious," Winnie Finney interrupted him, still beaming. "Doctor Fabrice will be with you as soon as possible."

The last thing David saw of him, before the door clicked shut, was a cheerfully winking eye. The music faded but did not altogether disappear. It sounded like the voice of an alien insect caught in the mazes of his ear.

David and Harley were now in a pale-blue room with tightly shut blue doors in three of its walls. Four chairs, upholstered in blue linen, were placed precisely around a low, glass table, spread with magazines in various languages.

In one corner of the room stood a television set which looked far too massive to show anything as light-hearted as soap operas or sitcoms. In the opposite corner was a bench which supported a water dispenser with a plastic tap protruding from it and a coffee machine with paper cups beside it.

David suddenly became aware of just how thirsty he was. He moved towards it to get himself a drink. Harley, though, leaped to test the door.

"There's no handle," he said in disbelief. "We can't get out."

"Did you think they'd let you wander around?" asked a voice – a girl's voice.

And there she was. The girl they had seen in the garage doorway. It was hard to be sure of anything in a place like this, but David was sure she had not been in the room when they first came into it.

Chapter Seven
Watching TV

"HOW DID YOU get in?" asked Harley.

"I've been waiting for you," she answered. "I knew they'd bring you here."

"No, but how *did* you get in?" persisted Harley.

"Oh, I can come and go," she answered.

She was still wearing her big, round, dark glasses, and still hugging the long, black jacket around her, almost as if she were cold. This made David register how *very* warm it was down here. The girl's bare legs vanished into black Doc Martens.

"Just tell us," said Harley. "How do we get out? I mean, if we *have* to."

The girl smiled. She had very white teeth, pointed and foxy.

"How did you get *in?*" she asked, mimicking Harley, but not unkindly.

"We got into a car which . . . which wasn't ours," Harley said.

"Oh, *that* car!" the girl replied, nodding and taking a packet of chewing gum from her coat pocket.

"We sort of *borrowed* it. Well, actually it borrowed *us*," said David, watching her pop a piece of gum into her mouth, though she did not offer any to either of them. She wore black leather, fingerless gloves.

"Wow! Isn't technology wonderful?" she said, not expecting an answer.

"Is the door behind you unlocked?" asked Harley. "Is that the way out?"

"In the end it is," the girl said. She spoke in a careless voice, but there was something strange about her expression. And then she opened her mouth but, though she seemed to struggle to speak, no words came. "I–I–I–I . . ." she stammered, then stopped struggling. "I don't seem to be able to tell you much," she said at last, blinking rapidly and speaking easily once more. "You'll have to guess."

"Do you work here?" Harley asked, while David stared at her, unable to understand what someone who looked like a streetpunk could possibly be doing in such a high-tech place.

"I do, at present," she said. "I'll be moving on when I finish my assignment."

"What *is* your assignment —" David began to ask, but Harley interrupted him.

"So, why can't you tell us much?" he cried. "Is it top secret or something?"

"I just can't," she said. "There's some law against it. I have to fight the laws all the time just to be here."

"Can you answer my questions?" David asked her.

"If you ask the right question. Well, you're halfway there whether I answer it or not," replied the girl.

"Have we just got to sit here and wait?" Harley cried irritably.

"Are you bored?" she asked.

"No," said Harley. "That's not the point –" But she interrupted him.

"Because if you *are* bored, Jack, you should find something to entertain yourselves." Her head turned a little so that her dark glasses appeared to focus on the television set in the corner. "Why not watch a soapie?" Her voice was light, almost playful, as if she were asking a riddle. "Better than nothing!"

David moved over to the set, then glanced back at her. She nodded once. Encouraged, he pressed the little button that said "Power". The screen sprang to life.

The image that formed was not in colour, but it was not in black and white either. The shadows and darker details were various shades of blue.

What they saw was an empty, curving corridor, perhaps the very one along which they had walked themselves only ten minutes earlier. They stared expectantly, but the corridor remained empty. No doors opened. Nothing happened.

"Bor-ing!" said the girl half-chanting. "Change channels."

"How?" David asked, but as he spoke he saw what looked like a programme selector sitting on top of the set. He snatched it up and clicked the single button.

Immediately, the corridor faded but other shapes came crowding through it as it disappeared. The screen now showed a scene that seemed familiar. Ten blue and white people were moving in a complicated reel through a room filled with equipment. And, there on the screen, David could make out ranks of other screens, crossed and recrossed by blips, wavy lines and tight scribbles of light.

"That's a *hospital*, isn't it?" cried Harley incredulously. "I mean, that's an operating room."

"It could be a tree hospital," suggested the girl. "What do you reckon?"

"Tell us then, if you're so smart," said Harley. He and David both looked from her to the screen, then back to her once more. She frowned and opened her mouth but, for the second time, she choked and no words came.

"Find out for yourselves," she said at last, stepping back with an indifferent shrug. "It's your funeral." Then she laughed as if she had made a joke.

David pressed the programme selector a second time. The image on the screen faded as another came through it, and to begin with he could not quite understand what he was seeing, though at the same time he felt he knew it well. Two figures were standing and staring at a screen. The backs were familiar, and surely the chairs . . . that table spread with magazines . . . David turned to check the magazines on the table beside him. Harley yelped.

"It's you!" he said. David looked quickly back at the screen but, as he turned his head, the image on the screen turned too, so he did not – could not – meet his own eyes.

"It's *us*, isn't it?" Harley said, and shivered. David found he was shivering as well.

"There must be a camera somewhere," he said, staring up at the ceiling. "Look! In that corner!" He pointed up at a corner. "That black thing like a round eye. They're spying on us."

"Monitoring you," said the girl. "They call it 'monitoring'. It sort of suggests they're taking care of you. And they *will* take care of you too . . . if you're not more careful than they are, that is."

David rapidly pressed the button once more.

This time they were looking into a large, tiled room lined along two walls with a continuous row of stainless-steel sinks, taps and steel refrigerators. Two steel tables resembling operating tables stood in the centre of the room, but there was nothing like the crowding of the expensive equipment that had taken up so much space in the operating theatre.

The third wall, only partly visible, seemed to be lined with the ends of steel drawers, all tightly closed. In one corner David had the impression of an area screened with plastic screens. It reminded him of something he had seen somewhere. However, before he could organize his memory, the screen went blank then filled with flickering snow.

"Hang on a bit!" said Harley. "Let me see that room again."

"It switched itself off," said David, pressing the button over and over again.

"Override command," said the girl. "Old Doctor Fabricate's trying to come through." And she chuckled a strange, dark chuckle.

A very different sort of picture began forming on the screen. They were now seeing, in full television colour, an office with a big well-ordered desk and a well-ordered man sitting behind it.

"Good evening," said the man. He spoke with some sort of accent, but David could not guess which country it suggested. "I am Doctor Fabrice. I think you were told to expect me. Now, listen carefully, because I am going to tell you what to do next."

Chapter Eight
Orders from Dr Fabrice

DR FABRICE WAS looking at them with severely scientific attention.

"I know you must be alarmed by your situation, but you have no cause to worry. In two minutes the door to the left of this screen will slide open. Go into the room beyond. You will find clean clothes next to the shower. You will then be moving into a germ-free system which we need to maintain, so after you have showered, please put on the uniform provided."

"I'm not dressing in any uniform," muttered Harley. He spoke softly.

"Failure to comply with this ruling will result in coercion," Dr Fabrice went on in a voice without emotion. "After you have gone through the process of disinfection, you will be interviewed and appropriately classified. Do remember you are here entirely by your own choice, and be co-operative."

The screen went blank once more, and one of the doors opened invitingly.

"I suppose we'd better go," David said

uncertainly. He turned to look at the girl and was filled, once more, with the peculiar feeling of having *missed out* on something – something important.

"When we saw ourselves on that screen . . ." He hesitated, and she raised her eyebrows at him. "Where *were* you?" he asked her. "You were right beside us, but the camera didn't seem to see you."

"Oh well, maybe I know enough about this place to keep out of the reach of cameras," she answered. "There are spots in every room they miss. Or maybe I have a secret skill, and just don't *show up*." And she laughed to herself.

"What's your name?" David asked, looking back over his shoulder even as he stepped through the door.

"Quinta!" she said. "What's yours?"

The door slid shut before he could answer. There was no going back.

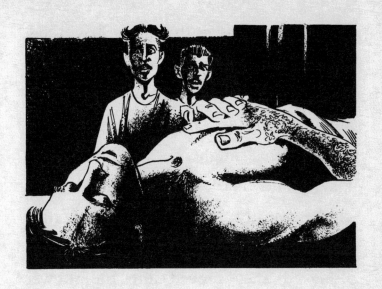

Chapter Nine
"There's no waking up"

QUINTA! THOUGHT DAVID. *Where's Quinta?*
That was what the graffiti on the wall in
Forbes Street had asked.

"Harley . . ." he began, and then fell
silent.

They were confronted by a series of

four shower alcoves that made David feel as if he were a sheep about to be dipped against his will. Anxious to seem mature and responsible, and to impress any cameras that might be watching them, David and Harley both folded their clothes neatly – something that they never did at home.

Naked, they moved into the shower alcoves waiting for them. But as they entered the showers, the doors closed behind them, clicking and locking in what was now a familiar fashion. And as the doors closed, what had appeared to be the back walls slid aside.

First Harley, then David came out – dripping and trembling – into a tiny room, tiled in blue and white, and without a single window.

There was a hiss. A warm, greenish spray fell from sprinklers in the ceiling above them. The room smelled of antiseptic.

"They're disinfecting us," said Harley, outraged. "What's going on?"

"He told us we would be disinfected," David replied. "That Doctor Fabrice, I mean." His voice sounded calm, but his head was spinning with amazement. *Quinta!* he was thinking. *Quinta!* She had, apparently, disappeared from Forbes Street. Could she have taken that car just as they had taken it? How long had she actually *been* here?

A door hummed open. Another pale-blue room. David glanced at the corners of the ceiling. Yes! There was the round black eye of a camera. Someone was watching – still watching. Someone was *monitoring* them. Pale-blue towels and clothes waited on a steel bench.

"Dresses!" yelled Harley in outrage.

"Gowns!" said David. "Hospital gowns. At least they're blue, not pink!"

"I'm not wearing a thing like that," said Harley. "It'll show my bum."

"No it won't! Well, not quite. And I want to get this over and done with," David said wearily, though the short gown did make him feel silly and defenceless. The door at the end of the room opened on cue. They walked through and found themselves in the office they had first seen on the television set.

The man behind the desk looked at them pleasantly enough.

"So!" he said mildly. "You stole a car and here you are."

"We weren't really stealing it," mumbled Harley.

"Just borrowing it?" suggested Dr Fabrice a little sarcastically. "Well, it's all very regrettable, but nothing we can't fix. It will take time. After all, you've pushed your way into a private establishment."

"I thought Willesden Forest was run by the government," Harley protested.

"Private in the sense that we don't encourage anyone to come here except by invitation," the doctor said. "Work goes on here which must be protected. We do have competitors, you know."

"May I ring my mother – just to let her know I am safe?" asked David.

"Certainly not," Dr Fabrice replied calmly.

"She'll be off her head with worry," David cried.

"You should have thought of her before you got into the car," said Dr Fabrice in rather a bored voice. "However, you're lucky in one way. We don't want to prosecute, but we *will* need to monitor you for a short term. Goodness knows what problems you have brought in with you, and you may even have suffered some contamination. We must check you out – not that we actually want the extra work."

"Contamination? You mean *viruses* might have got into us?" cried Harley, dismayed. "Dangerous ones?"

"Let's hope not," Dr Fabrice said calmly. "It *is* just possible. I'll give you the appropriate shots in a moment. In the meantime, there are a few questions I'd like you to answer. Let's begin with your names and your dates of birth."

Harley and David answered question after question. What illnesses had they had? Did they have any allergies? Were either of them taking any medication? Did either or both of them take drugs? Were either of them on insulin? Or steroids? Did they drink? Had either of them ever had any heart disease? Had either of them ever had any injections into the heart? Were there any illnesses in their families . . . illnesses which they might have inherited?

The questions went on and on. David and Harley answered and answered until the room faded around them and they wilted in their chairs.

Finally, Dr Fabrice rang a bell. A dark young woman in a nurse's uniform came in, pushing a small trolley. She did not so much as glance at them. It was as if they did not exist.

"We need a blood sample from each of you," said Dr Fabrice. "It won't hurt."

"What's all this in aid of?" demanded Harley.

"It's for your own good," Dr Fabrice repeated. "It's not worth explaining. You wouldn't understand why."

His voice was soft and calm, but there was something unpleasant – even insulting – about it too.

"We're not stupid," David said, watching his blood climb through the needle and into the tube the nurse was holding.

Dr Fabrice glanced at him.

"Oh, are you not?" he asked. "Then why are you here? You were not invited."

"OK, so it was a dumb thing to do," David said. "But everyone does something stupid, sooner or later."

"A charming theory," replied Dr Fabrice, smiling coldly.

"Hang on a bit," David began, suddenly wanting to argue.

But Harley began jiggling nervously beside him, muttering, "Shut up! Shut up!" under his breath. Then he said aloud, "We're sorry. OK? We'll go away and never bother you again . . . never say another word. Promise!"

"Of course, I do believe you," said Dr Fabrice in his wintry voice. "Of course, I entirely believe you'll walk away and never so much as *whisper* about anything you may have seen here. Two boys as honest as you would stick to your promises. All the same, the foolish rules insist that you sign these forms – legal agreements to remain silent about your little misadventure. This is a research facility, you know. And these are the days of international industrial espionage. So, sign these forms, and then we can hold you legally responsible for any rumours."

"Do you think we're spies?" asked Harley incredulously. "But we're . . . we're *kids*."

"Many people of your age are well able to handle computers, for example," said Dr Fabrice. "Sign the release forms now, and later, after we have checked with our lawyer, you will be sent home."

"How much later?" asked David. "I mean, my mother . . . please let me ring her."

"I'm afraid not," said Dr Fabrice, watching as Harley signed the pink form without bothering to read it. Then it was David's turn. As he scribbled his signature, he heard Harley yawning behind him and knew exactly how he felt. It seemed as if they were signing-off after a long and dangerous job, free at last to feel properly tired, even sleepy.

Dr Fabrice took the forms and put them in a basket on one side of his desk.

"I can offer you a bed until . . . oh, until the morning shift comes on," he said. "I suggest you sleep. Our night staff will wash and clean your clothes for you."

Dr Fabrice sounded so *sure* of what must be done.

The worst was over. Sleep would somehow make the next few hours come and go in less than a second. David and Harley looked at each other, half nodding, half shrugging.

Sitting beside his desk, Dr Fabrice had seemed imposing; on his feet he was revealed as short and squat. The boys followed him out into the corridor, and once more music came to meet them. It did more than meet them . . . it attacked them.

To David it sounded as if it were exactly the same music that had been playing when they had first stepped out of the lift into this pale-blue curve. For some reason it made him think yet again of horror films . . . of mad, hooded figures sitting before double keyboards, with stops and pipes sprouting like fungi from solid rock.

Dr Fabrice opened a door. David found he was looking into yet another blue room, but this time he saw whiteness – two white beds, so soft and pure that a sigh of pleasure escaped him at the sight. After the shower, the disinfecting and then the question-and-answer session, he felt soft and pure himself, all natural dirt washed away and all responsibility passed on.

He and Harley let Dr Fabrice herd them into the room, and David, glancing upwards, checked for any lensed eye that might be scanning the room. Yes! There it was, still watching him. But, so what? All it would see over the next few hours would be two boys sleeping, free of care.

And then Harley cried out in terror.

David's gaze skidded across Harley's

gaping face to the bed on the left-hand side of the narrow room. It had been empty. It *had*! Yet now there was someone in it.

A young man lay under the crisp white cover, apparently asleep. David thought, in the first dizzy second, that he was wearing long, fingerless, blue lace gloves. Then he understood that the hands (folded left over right) were covered in intricate tattoos that reached up as far as the young man's elbows. His forearms writhed with flowers, naked girls half-covered by their own flowing hair, and spiralling serpents. The skin showing between the lines looked yellowish and translucent, the flesh like rapidly clearing water.

In just a minute, thought David in terror, I'll be able to see right through him to the sheet beneath. The room seemed to fall away, and for a moment he believed, with woolly astonishment, that he was about to faint. I can't! I mustn't, he thought, twisting around yet again to stare at Dr Fabrice, standing behind him.

For a moment Dr Fabrice appeared to have some ghastly owl perched on his shoulder. Familiar dark glasses were staring back at David from just behind the doctor, who seemed entirely unaware of either the young man in the bed, or of Quinta, his unexpected shadow.

Harley screamed aloud. A horrid scarlet had begun pumping up between the man's fingers, spreading over the thin, blue border of the white sheet . . . surely not the same sheet they had seen when he first glanced into the room? How could something like a blue border be as horrifying as the terrible spreading stain?

"Blood!" Harley shouted.

"Now, then," Dr Fabrice said, staring at them in irritation. "Don't make a stupid fuss. Sleep . . . just sleep . . . and we'll wake you for breakfast."

Behind him, Quinta straightened as if she were a puppet jerked upwards by unseen strings. Tilting her head back, she howled.

"Run! Run now! There's no waking up! No breakfast! Hide! Hi–ide! Run and hide!"

Dr Fabrice *heard* the owl on his shoulder. Suddenly he knew she was there. His jaw dropped. He turned. Quinta actually smiled at him as if they were old friends. His eyes were only centimetres away from her glasses. As David and Harley, acting together, pushed past him, a dreadful sound forced its way out of Dr Fabrice . . . not just a groan of fear, but the agony of a man having his brain invisibly torn and twisted inside his head.

First Harley, then David scrambled out of the room, pelting as fast as they could along the pale-blue curving corridor, even though they knew of no safe place to run to. It was as if they had been practising that fast take-off for a long time.

Somewhere behind the perpetual music, something began screaming. Someone's torturing a cat, thought David in horror, but the scream rose and fell too evenly for true pain. What he was hearing was a siren.

Glancing back over his shoulder, he glimpsed Dr Fabrice crawling along the floor of the blue corridor, his head hanging down almost to the floor, like a mechanical toy with a broken neck. Then he collapsed and lay still. Somehow David knew he would never get up again.

And now David felt the vibration of pursuit. Feet were running from somewhere, pounding towards them. Grabbing a handle on the nearest door, he twisted it madly. Miraculously the door opened, and both he and Harley bolted sideways into darkness, pulling it shut behind them.

It clicked in such a conclusive way that David immediately knew they were locked in, and the thought of being locked in this terrible, unknown, *black* place made him giddy with fear. As he slowly sank down on his trembling haunches, burying his face in his hands, he was aware of Harley collapsing beside him.

"He was dead . . . that boy was *dead*," Harley mumbled. David suspected he might be weeping in the dark.

"Shhh!" he whispered. Feet thumped rapidly past the door. He put out his hand and touched Harley's arm. "He can't have been *dead*," he said, trying to be sensible and comforting at the same time. "Dead men don't bleed."

"He was *dead*," repeated Harley obstinately. "And not only that . . ."

He stopped talking. David did not want to think about what Harley had started to say. Before entering the room they had both looked in at the beds, and those beds had certainly been empty. As if it were feeding on David's fear, the music grew louder and louder. The darkness rang with it, and David felt that he must be ringing with it too.

Chapter Ten
Organ Music

THEN IT FADED again.

"I hate that music," panted David.

"Bach," whispered Harley.

"Bark?" David turned his head towards Harley but could not see anything but blackness. "Woof woof?"

"Bach! You know! Bach, the composer! *Toccata and Fugue in D minor.* They've been playing that *and* the *Passacaglia and Fugue in C minor* ever since we came in here. *And* Mozart! *Fantasia in F minor.* Nothing but organ music!"

It vaguely surprised David that Harley might know about things like *passacaglias* and organ music. But he supposed he had probably heard a lot of music before his mother left.

"What *happened*?" Harley asked, sounding like someone struggling back out of a nightmare into ordinary life.

"Quinta yelled 'Run!' and we ran," David said. He took a deep breath. "Harley – you know that street where we found the car? Forbes Street?"

Harley nodded.

"Quinta's name was sprayed on the wall. *Where's Quinta?* it said. Well, Quinta's *here*. But what's she *doing* here?"

He felt Harley shrug in the darkness. "What are *we* doing here?" he replied.

"It's not the same," said David. "Not yet, anyway!" he added, shuddering as he spoke. "We've just arrived, and she must have been here for a long time. She knows her way around."

"She knew about the car," Harley agreed.

"We were tricked here. That car was a trap," said David. "I think it's sent to Forbes Street to *catch* people. Remember what Winnie Finney said about taking it on its first run? Perhaps that's why people are saying Forbes Street is haunted. But what's it all for? I mean, who'd spend a million dollars on a car just to catch you and me. Every now and then I feel I almost *know* what's going on, and then it all fades away before I can really grab hold of it."

He waved his hand. "I mean, when you mentioned organ music a minute ago I felt you'd said something really important – but I don't know *why* it seemed important. Ghostly!"

"Ghosts! Don't go on about your ghosts, or you'll have me believing in them too," said Harley. His voice was still trembling but with every word he sounded more and more like his usual self.

"Stop telling me I believe in ghosts," said David angrily. "I *don't* believe in ghosts. I never have!" (Until now, he added to himself.) "All the same . . ." he began, and stopped. It was mad, but he *had* to say it. "Talking about ghosts . . ."

"Yeah! Yeah!" Harley interrupted him quickly, leaping to his feet and accidentally striking something that rang like a bell made of tin. "Where are the lights?" David could hear him scrabbling around the wall beside the door. "Here we are . . . I think!"

The burst of white light made David feel he had been struck in the face.

They were standing in a large, bright room, hemmed around by stainless steel benches, sinks and steel-doored refrigerators. The floor and even the walls were covered with white tiles, though one wall was patched with what seemed to be big steel drawers. In the centre of the room stood two spotless steel tables with channels in them, and beyond these was an alcove which also seemed to be tiled, but which was closed off by pleated plastic screens.

David had never been in this room before. All the same, he recognized it. It had appeared earlier on the closed circuit of the waiting-room television set. He looked up at the ceiling and, sure enough, there was the black eye, familiar by now, staring down at them. David remembered that the plastic screens had been on the edge of the eye's field of sight, and he remembered Quinta saying that there were some spots in every room which the camera could not see.

"Let's hide behind those screens," he said. "Come on."

"Why would anyone come all the way out here for an operation?" Harley asked.

"I mean – why *would* they?"

He had obviously been looking around the room and puzzling over it.

"I don't know," said David, as they edged uneasily towards the screens. "And anyway, this isn't an operating theatre."

"It must be. Those tables . . ."

"It's a mortuary," said David. "I've seen them on television." He set his teeth, grimacing as he glanced around him, and lowered his voice in case he disturbed something hidden. "They pull out one of those drawers and there's your ex-wife, or someone they've dredged up out of the river," he whispered.

"A mortuary?" Harley muttered back, his voice alive with new alarm. "Why would they want one out here?"

David edged behind the screens,

listening to the music.

"Organ music," he said. His teeth which had been clenched until now began to chatter. "Organ music," he repeated. "And something done secretly! I think people come here because they don't want to go on long waiting lists at ordinary hospitals."

As he spoke, they found themselves behind the screens, facing an arched doorway and a little room where two people lay in bed.

These people were alone but not unattended. Each bed was so surrounded by machines and screens that the room was like the setting for a science-fiction game. The occupants of the beds lay like dead people, but David knew from watching hospital series on television that the looping lines on the screens showed some sort of life was in progress.

"Just think!" he said slowly, staring at the screens. "Suppose Doctor Fabrice has been doing some sort of secret medical service for rich people . . . liver transplants or something like that. Sometimes people have to wait a long time for a new liver." Then his mind made another jump. "And suppose—"

"Shut up!" Harley cried out. "I don't want to suppose any more about anything."

For the patient in the nearest bed was the young man they had already seen in the bed further down the hall. There was no doubt about it. Though he now had a mask over most of his face and various tubes and wires plastered into his neck and arms, the blue tattoos on his hands and forearms were unmistakable. His skin was pale but lacked the horrid transparency that it had had earlier.

David felt suddenly sure that the young man in front of them was real. Here, he lay unconscious. But some mysterious part of him was free and had materialized in front of them, giving them a kind of warning. And in the next bed . . . Though filled with horror at his own guesses, David felt he must see *who* was under the sheet, wired into the machines. He believed it would be Quinta.

"Don't look!" said Harley.

And then they heard a faint, familiar sound. Beyond the screens the door had opened.

"Are you there?" someone asked in a

loud whisper. "You can come out now."

Harley put a finger to his lips. But feet were crossing the tiled floor.

"Don't be worried," said a voice. "I'm on *your* side."

Someone peered around the edge of one of the screens, and beamed at them.

"Oh, there you are!" said a voice. It was Winnie Finney.

Chapter Eleven

"Rubbish off the street"

"A LOT OF people are looking for you two," he remarked. "I thought I'd join in the hunt. You seem to be causing a bit of trouble, and I have a soft spot for troublemakers. I was a bit of a tearaway myself, way back when."

"Something's going on," said David. "Something . . . something really freaky."

Winnie Finney looked around the room, rather as if he too found it unpleasant.

"After all, it *is* a research establishment," he said, half to himself. "No wonder people like you and me find it all a bit strange. At the same time – you're right – it is a little bit *bothering*, isn't it? And I can't believe you kids mean any harm. So if we get to my room you can hide out there, until the staff – the daytime staff – come on duty. You'll have more chance of getting away when there are a lot of people around."

David could have kissed him. He sounded so ordinary and easy-going . . . so *reliable*.

89

"I'll check the corridor," said Winnie Finney. "The lift's almost directly opposite."

The boys watched as he opened the door, peered right, peered left, and then beckoned them forward.

"Are you ready? Then, follow me! Now!"

Sliding furtively after him, a little way along the blue corridor, they stopped beside a dark-blue grille. Winnie Finney pressed a button. First the grille, and then the door behind it, hissed open. The three of them piled through, Winnie Finney pressing buttons. The lift shot up (though how *far* up, David could not tell), then came to a stop. The door slid open once more, and they stepped out on to a deep-red carpet. The warm colour was a relief after all that chilly blue.

"My office is along here," said Winnie Finney. "And no one bothers to bother me. I'm the mechanic . . . the odd-jobs man. So come and sit down and have something to eat. Then you can tell me what's going on."

"I'm starving," said Harley, amazing David once more. He couldn't imagine ever wanting to eat anything again. The mere thought of meat made his stomach heave painfully. He was thirsty, but all he wanted to drink was water. More than anything else, he wanted things to be pure and simple.

Winnie Finney led the way along the red carpet to a polished door which opened into a book-lined room, worn and homely. He had an untidy desk, an overflowing waste-paper basket, and an old-fashioned electric-bar heater. There was a table in one corner of the room on which sat an old electric jug. Shelves with cups and saucers, and a tin that looked as if it might hold biscuits, rose behind it.

"Sit!" said Winnie Finney, as if they were dogs. "Just sit for a moment. Are you cold?" He leaned behind his desk to turn on the heater. "We'll be as warm as toast in a minute."

David slumped gratefully into a cane chair filled with soft, floppy cushions.

"I'll lock the door," said Winnie Finney. "Then no one will be able to burst in on us." And he did.

"Now, tell me everything", he said to David, "while I make coffee."

"Well," David began, "we were walking home – hours ago it was –"

"Last night," put in Harley.

"Whenever that was," said David, looking at the windows. Between a slit in the drawn curtains he saw what looked like a genuine night-time darkness. They must be on ground level once more.

Between them they told him about the car with the winking seductive key, and the way they had been carried along the motorway and over the hill. As they talked, Winnie Finney made the coffee and set the low table with biscuits and three wide, flowery cups. He poured coffee into the cups, then, looking at them almost roguishly, took a silver hip flask from his pocket and added a slug of ginger-coloured liquid.

"We're all men of the world," he said. "We need something for shock. Help yourselves to milk and sugar."

He sat back in what was obviously his special chair. It had lions' heads on the arms, but he covered them with his wide hands so that the lions seemed to snarl out from between his fingers.

By now they were talking about Quinta, interrupting one another as they talked, filled with the relief of passing on their fears, and the pleasure of being in an ordinary room filled with ordinary things. In between talking, they drank their coffee, enjoying the taste, and the feeling of grown-up, manly fellowship.

"So this isn't just a forestry place," explained David. "Well, it might be, but there's something *else* going on here." He held his coffee cup in both hands, enjoying its warmth and comfort.

"Transplants!" announced Harley, as proudly as if he had worked it all out for himself. David looked at him in surprise, for he had not been at all sure that Harley had even listened to his theory. "They pick up people on the streets, and David thinks they use them for spare parts. I mean, those people probably just disappear. No one's going to report that car missing. In a way, it doesn't exist."

Winnie Finney's smile vanished.

"It *is* possible," he said. "I designed that car, you know. My main work is unmanned machines – machines that are used in hard-access forestry areas. The car was a hobby – a treat. And I must admit I set it up, but once I'd solved the problems I rather lost interest. And it's true that some of the people I see around here from time to time don't look like tree lovers."

"What do tree lovers look like?" said Harley with a faint grin, his first for quite a while.

David shifted his cup of coffee to his left hand, putting out his right for another biscuit. But his right hand was reluctant to move. It went halfway towards the table, then flopped on to his knee. At the same time, the coffee cup fell from his fingers. He had the illusion that it had actually passed through them.

Alarmed, he turned, trying to check on Harley and found that all his movements had become enormously slow. Slowly his eyes wandered back to stare, swimmingly, in front of him once more, and he found himself looking into the face of Winnie Finney, beaming across his own untouched cup of coffee.

"Oh no!" David tried to say . . . but he could not say it. A thick, wordless sound forced its way between his lips, but all sense was trapped inside his head.

"Ah, I see you've caught on," said Winnie Finney, leaning forward and peering intently into David's set face. "You *know*, don't you?" His mouth stretched into an even wider smile.

Harley was looking slowly from one to the other of them.

"What's . . . wrong?" he asked, and his voice sounded distant, slow and smudgy.

David struggled to reply but found he could not. His coffee cup was almost empty.

Winnie Finney rose briskly and stood over them.

"There are so many worthless people

97

around," he said, suddenly transformed into quite a different man – beaming, but no longer kindly. "Yet these trashy people have perfectly good organs . . . lungs . . . hearts . . . livers . . . while worthwhile citizens, people who have lived good productive lives, lovely youngsters with a world of promise ahead of them, find themselves breaking down simply by getting older or through some silly accident. Properly functioning organs should not be wasted on scum who are going to vandalize themselves with drink and drugs.

"Do you know that, each year in the USA alone, five thousand organs perfectly suitable for transplantation are buried or burned, at a time when there are twenty-four thousand people in the States all desperate for kidney transplants? Only ten thousand of them will get what they need . . . what they would *treasure*."

He wandered across his little office, studied a barometer on the wall and tapped it delicately. Then he turned and looked over at them once more.

"The two young men in the room off the morgue are what we call 'brain dead'," he said. "They would certainly die if we disconnected them from the life-support systems you saw, but we are keeping them alive - technically alive. We need them . . . fresh, you see. They don't deserve to live. *They* didn't respect themselves, so why should *I* bother to respect them?" Winnie Finney laughed.

"But so many organs have a very brief useful life, once they are taken from the parent body. A heart should be transplanted within – oh, say, six to eight hours. A lung may last for twelve hours. Of course there are parts of the body that *can* be preserved. Freshly frozen skin can last over three years. So can bone marrow. Heart valves last for five years and so does cartilage of the knee.

"We'll use those young men with far more respect and dignity than they would have used themselves, though comparatively little of them will be usable. Their corneas from their *eyes*, you know, their lungs, perhaps some sections of skin. Now, *you* – provided you don't have leukaemia or any AIDS risk factors, or anything of that kind – at your age you are a treasure trove."

He frowned at them, looking a little troubled.

"You see, once you're here there's no going back," he cried irritably. "Why on earth were you stupid enough to get into the car? What were you doing in *Forbes* Street, of all disgusting places?"

David could not answer. But someone answered for him.

"I was a Forbes Street kid," said a voice . . . Quinta's voice. Yet she was not in the room. Her voice sounded only in David's head. "I was trash . . . or that's what *he* would have called me. But I was *tough* trash. Too tough for him! He hasn't been able to see *me* off. I'm still hanging round, waiting for my chance."

Winnie Finney seemed quite unaware that Quinta was speaking.

"There are better people than you who can use your corneas, your livers and tendons. You'll have fulfilled lives that way. After all, it *is* immortality of a kind," he said.

He picked up his phone.

"Call me! Go on! Call me!" said Quinta's voice. "Make him *see* me."

David could not speak, but he shouted with a soundless voice he discovered within himself.

"Quinta! Quinta!"

"I have with me the two specimens we mislaid," Winnie Finney was saying into the phone. "They're unharmed except for a drug that will work its way through their systems quite harmlessly. But we've been a little complacent, haven't we? A little careless." His words were mild but his voice was menacing. He was being very nasty to someone. "We must be *careful*," he said, and, if he could have shuddered, David would have shuddered.

Behind Winnie Finney the air was swirling and thickening. Somehow, Quinta formed herself out of nothing. Of course! David thought. She really is a ghost. She isn't on any life-support system.

At the same time, he knew he definitely did not believe in ghosts. He had never believed in them, even as a little boy.

"Think *at* him! *Think* at him," Quinta's voice said, echoing somehow as if she were speaking inside his brain and as if his skull were empty of everything except her. "They can't monitor thoughts. They can't *transplant* them. Tell him *he's* the blemished one! Sullied! Disfigured! Give him the *words*! He knows them already,

103

but he grins and crushes them. Set them free! You can! You can!"

David felt like someone looking through a dreadful looking-glass and seeing a monster on the other side.

Blemished! Disfigured! Sullied! he thought, and felt the thoughts flow through Quinta towards Winnie Finney. And then, within himself, he heard music – the same music that had haunted the corridor outside.

"Yes! Yes! Call a team together!" Winnie Finney was saying. But then he stiffened, dropped the phone and swung around to stare at David.

"Oh no!" he said softly. His words broke off, as if the chords of music, swelling in his head, had shocked him.

Harley! thought David. Harley was

remembering the music into existence, and using it to strike at Winnie Finney.

Disfigured! he thought, as ferociously as he could, and Winnie Finney flung up his arm like a man warding off a blow. As he did this it seemed he became aware at last of Quinta, there beside him.

"You!" he shouted. "You're dead. And don't look at me! I lost a daughter – a good sweet girl, worth a hundred of you. I've helped humanity – those that deserved it."

Quinta was looking at him fixedly. David could only see the red stubble on the back of her head. It was like looking at a skull sprinkled with cayenne pepper.

"You were paid though, weren't you?" she said to Winnie Finney. "For helping humanity, I mean. And anyhow, how can I possibly be looking at you?" Saying this, she let go of her black coat in order to tilt her glasses up so that she and Winnie Finney could, apparently, be eye to eye.

Winnie Finney screamed.

"Funny though! I can see right through you!" Quinta said, and laughed.

He screamed again.

Someone was banging on the door, but Winnie Finney himself had locked it and was in no condition to unlock it now.

As David watched, it seemed to him a slow, dark slug crawled over the curve of Quinta's cheek. As if she were about to answer a question he had asked, she turned her head towards him and as light moved across the slug he saw it was a dark, thick, red colour. Then, with her dark glasses still tilted up on her forehead, she looked directly at the boys.

Quinta had no eyes. They had been cut out of her head. Below these ragged caves her smile was horrifying.

"Rubbish off the street," screamed Winnie Finney. He had shrunk back from her until his desk stopped him from going any further. Now he slowly crouched, his arms over his head. "I gave your eyes to someone who used them well – an artist who paints wonderful pictures."

Quinta laughed.

"I don't hold it against you," she said. "How can I? After all, you have my heart." Letting the top of her coat fall open, her bare chest was like some sort of winter seed pod cracked open and empty. "All my heart, and more besides." Suddenly, she wrenched the coat wide.

The whole body beneath it seemed to split open, tumbling tubes and pieces that nobody had wanted on to the floor between them.

Winnie Finney writhed and struggled, collapsing still further. It was as if air were escaping from him.

"Oh, what a piece of work is man," said Quinta. "Woman, too!"

Winnie Finney fell sideways, gasping as if he could not get enough air – as if he would never get air into his lungs ever again. His polished heels beat up and down against the floor, kicking over his rubbish basket. Crumpled paper spilled across the floor. His hands slapped the polished boards desperately. His gasping gave way to a kind of wet, dirty gurgling. At last he lay still.

Quinta carelessly patted her dark glasses back into place. Smoke was rising behind her. David thought it was part of her ghostliness – a special effect with dry ice.

"He could have done with a better heart himself, couldn't he?" she remarked. "I don't suppose I was much when I was alive, and probably the people who wound up with my eyes, my liver, my kidneys – all my bits – made better use of them than I would have. But I reckon you ought to offer your own eyes before you go volunteering other people's, don't you?

"I was determined to get him. But until you two walked in and I found someone who believed in ghosts, nothing worked. I really pulled myself together when you two came along. And I was able to call on Scag's ghost too. Scag's the guy with the tats. Fabrice and Finney did that to him — turned him into a desirable product hooked up to machinery so they could use pieces of him when they needed to. But they're both dead, and now I'm off. I don't know what comes next, and I don't care. Whatever it is, it'll be a change."

She sat down on the edge of the desk and, as Harley and David stared, she grew transparent and vanished. But the smoke did not disappear. Suddenly they realized that the papers on the floor were blazing. Winnie Finney had kicked the contents of the rubbish basket into his heater.

The basket itself was blazing, the desk was starting to burn. The room began to fill with smoke, and there was a nasty smell of melting plastic. David and Harley coughed and spluttered.

"We're going to die," Harley choked in David's ear. His voice sounded low and struggling as if he was talking in his sleep. Later, David could not be sure that Harley had really managed to say this. He might have thought it himself.

But as the smoke thickened and the flames leaped higher, overhead sprinklers came on. David toppled himself forward out of the chair, for he had read that in a burning building you should get as close to the floor as you can. Harley copied him. Water and smoke mingled in their nostrils.

We're going to die, thought David.

Then the door burst open. Men with extinguishers burst in. Feet trampled around them . . . stumbled over them. Someone grabbed David's shoulders and

began to tug him out of the room. And
then, just as he was being rescued, David
lost consciousness.

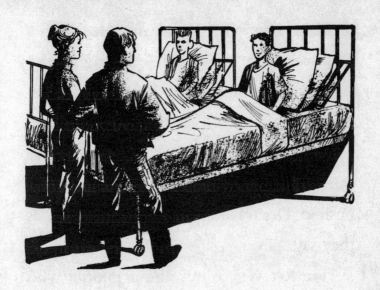

Chapter Twelve
Who Believes in Ghosts?

"DOCTOR FINNEY – YOUR friend, Winnie Finney – wasn't a *medical* doctor," said David's mother. "He was some sort of engineer specializing in very sophisticated automated machines for use in forestry operations. Unfortunately, something

113

terrible happened to him. He was a widower with one child — a daughter he adored — and this poor girl had a faulty heart. She was on a waiting list for a transplant operation. But while she was waiting, she died, and apparently her death pushed Doctor Finney over the edge, as they say."

"He felt very bitter about people who didn't deserve to live . . . in his opinion, at least," said David's father, standing between the boys' beds. "Criminals, for example, or people who were careless with their good health. Anyhow, when the overseas group bought a share of the Willesden Forest Research Centre, he made contact with some rather peculiar people . . . and, to cut a long story short, began running this part of a nasty business. The money came from an international syndicate. They *operated* . . ."

David exclaimed as if the word suddenly horrified him.

"I mean they really *did* operate. Sometimes here, sometimes in Australia, sometimes in Singapore. They had several bases. The medical teams came into the country as tourists and would wind up at the Willesden Forest Research Centre.

"Meanwhile, Winnie Finney developed his strange car, and he and Doctor Fabrice collected people off the street – people they thought would not be missed – killed them and used their spare parts for transplants. After all, their clientele were very rich and often very desperate – certainly not used to waiting for anything – least of all for something as necessary as a donated heart or liver. So the prices the syndicate charged were astronomical.

"They always worked within some existing business and used it as a cover. For instance, the building where you had your adventure was built and paid for by the syndicate, but if you had left the garage by the right-hand door of the two, you would have gone up in a lift and found yourselves in a section devoted to the development of bacteria genetically altered to attack forest predators without harming native birds. Quite legitimate, you see."

"When can we get out of hospital?" asked Harley. "Not that I'm in a hurry," he added quickly. His big sister had been to see him once but his father had not been in at all. David thought Harley must be feeling deserted.

"You're both well recovered from the drug Winnie Finney gave you in the coffee. We'll collect you both tomorrow," said David's father. He hesitated. "Actually, Harley, your mother is on her way back."

There was a little silence.

"What's *she* coming for?" Harley muttered at last.

"She was dreadfully upset when she heard about your adventure," said David's father. "I know it won't be *easy* for you, but I think you should try hard – very hard – to be nice to her. And we've arranged that you'll stay with us for a few days. I understand your father is having a hard time at work. At least, he's too busy to look after you properly."

117

"Ha ha!" said Harley. "He's sick of me. He wants a different sort of kid." David could see he was struggling not to cry. "I'd like to come, though," he added quickly. "And . . . and it'll be OK – seeing Mum again, I mean."

"It's because of her you knew about that organ music," said David. "And that music was partly what made Winnie Finney see Quinta."

"Quinta?" asked his father. David and Harley looked at one another and fell silent. The two brain-dead young men had been found in a room off the mortuary, but there had been no sign of any other victims. For some reason Quinta was a secret which could not be talked about . . . except between themselves.

"David . . ." Harley said, after David's

parents had gone home, hugging them both and promising to collect them as soon as possible. Harley almost never used David's name. Usually he just said, "Hey you!"

David looked over at him.

"She . . . she sort of saved our lives twice over, didn't she?" Harley said. "Quinta, I mean."

"Suppose so!" said David. "I think if we'd lain down in those beds and gone to sleep . . . well, we wouldn't ever have woken up again. First she stopped Doctor Fabrice, and then she stopped Winnie Finney."

"She sure did," said Harley, shuddering.

"Lucky for us the firemen were true forestry people . . . nothing to do with any international syndicate," sighed David.

"Lucky for us they called the police!" Harley exclaimed, but he was not really thinking about their escape. "I know all that. But listen! Before Quinta frightened Winnie Finney to death she said she could only be seen because we believed in ghosts, didn't she? She somehow worked *through* us."

"I *don't* believe in ghosts," sighed David. "I keep on telling you that. Well, I suppose I just might from now on, but I didn't believe in them last night. I've never believed in them."

Harley sighed as well.

"I do," he said simply. "I always have. I pretended I didn't, because people – you know, my father and sister and other people – always slung off at me."

David thought about this.

"Well," he said at last, speaking rather drowsily, "you believe in ghosts and I *read* about them. It's part of the same thing, I suppose."

But Harley did not answer. He had fallen asleep with his hair sticking up like the crest of a startled cockatoo.

And within another minute, David had fallen asleep too and, as he slept, his strong heart beat regularly, and his good lungs breathed smoothly. Every bit of him was working well. And he was so tired that no terrible dreams disturbed his sleeping.

The dreams would come later.